PAC

70
RIG

Amazing
Wolves
Dogs & Foxes

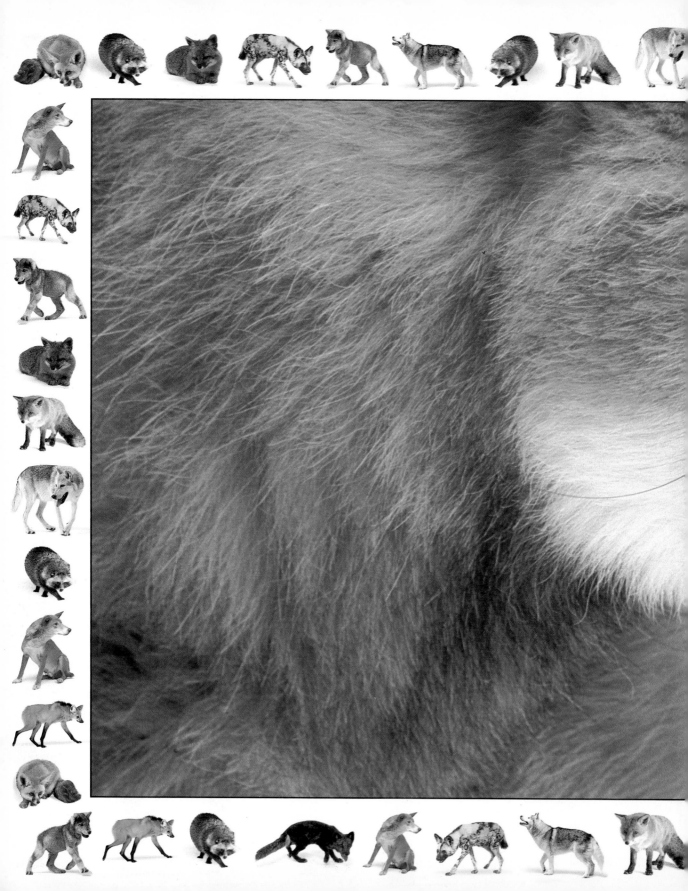

EYEWITNESS JUNIORS

Amazing
Wolves
Dogs & Foxes

WRITTEN BY
MARY LING

PHOTOGRAPHED BY
JERRY YOUNG

ALFRED A. KNOPF • NEW YORK

DK
Conceived and produced by
Dorling Kindersley Limited

Project editor Louise Pritchard
Art editor Ann Cannings
Senior editor Helen Parker
Senior art editor Jacquie Gulliver
Production Louise Barratt

Illustrations by Angelika Elsbach, Julie Anderson,
John Hutchinson, Dan Wright
Animals supplied by Trevor Smith's Animal World,
Duisburger Zoo, Germany
Editorial consultants The staff of the Natural History Museum, London
Special thanks to Carl Gombrich and Kate Raworth for research

This is a Borzoi Book published by Alfred A. Knopf, Inc.

Library of Congress Cataloging in Publication Data
Ling, Mary
Amazing wolves, dogs & foxes / written by Mary Ling
photographed by Jerry Young.
p. cm. - (Eyewitness juniors; 16)
Includes index
Summary: Text and photographs introduce amazing members of the Canidae family,
including the dingo, the gray wolf, and the Arctic fox.
1. Foxes – Juvenile literature. 2. Dogs – Juvenile literature. 3. Wolves – Juvenile literature.
4. Canidae – Juvenile literature.
[1. Wolves. 2. Dogs. 3. Foxes. 4. Canidae.]
I. Young, Jerry, ill. II. Title. III. Title: Amazing wolves, dogs, and foxes. IV. Series.
QL737.C22L495 1991 599.74'442 – dc20 91-6514
ISBN 0-679-81521-X
ISBN 0-679-91521-4 (lib. bdg.)

Color reproduction by Colourscan, Singapore
Printed in Italy by A. Mondadori Editore, Verona

Contents

Running wild

The pet dog has about 35 wild relatives in the dog family. You have probably heard of the gray wolf, the red fox, the coyote, and the dingo. But have you ever heard of the raccoon dog or the dhole?

Hip joint muscles

Neck muscles

Shoulder muscles

Leg muscles

This dingo is about 2 feet high at the shoulder

Dog's body
Most dogs stand upright on fairly long legs. They have lots of muscles and a long tail and are covered in fur.

The young ones
Dogs usually have one group, or litter, of pups a year. One litter may contain two or three pups or as many as ten or twelve. The pups are looked after until they can hunt for themselves.

Diving dog
There is a wild member of the dog family in almost every part of the world – the Arctic, deserts, forests, and cities. Some can climb; others can swim. The bush dog of South America dives underwater!

Gone wild

Aborigines brought the dingo to Australia as a hunting companion long ago. Now the dingo is wild.

Pointed teeth for stabbing prey

Strong teeth for chewing

Snap happy

Dogs are carnivores, which means they eat meat. They have strong jaws and teeth for tearing, grinding, and chewing.

Face like a dog

As well as barking, dogs talk with their faces, tails, and bodies. These wolves are arguing, and the one on the right is saying, "You win!"

Packing them in

Many wild dogs live together in packs. There are strict rules within the pack, and every member knows its place.

Muddy paws

A dog cannot tuck away its blunt, sturdy nails the way a cat pulls in its claws. These wolf paw prints clearly show the nail marks in the mud.

Top dog

Wolves are the largest members of the dog family. There are two kinds of wolf – the gray wolf and the red wolf. Sadly, the red wolf is almost extinct.

Hungry to kill

Wolves hunt only when they are hungry. Most scary stories about wolves attacking people are not true. Healthy wolves do not attack humans unless they have a good reason.

On the run

Wolves are great runners and can keep up a steady pace for many hours. An American red wolf once ran for two weeks. It covered about 125 miles.

Stepping lively

Wolves usually trot from place to place or run in a way called loping. But in a chase they can reach speeds of up to 40 miles per hour in short bursts.

What big teeth!

The wolf's sharp teeth are ideal for catching and eating large animals such as deer or elk. But wolves also eat rabbits, snakes, insects, and even fruit!

Long, strong legs and long paws make running easy

Wolf power

Gray wolves can have black, white, or gray fur, depending on where they live. This male gray wolf is about 3 feet tall at the shoulder. Female wolves are usually slightly smaller than the males.

Wolves have a good sense of smell for sniffing out prey

Moonlighting

Stories are told of people who become wolves after dark and terrify their neighbors. These people are called werewolves, but don't worry – they are only make-believe!

Cry wolf

Many people are scared by the sound of wolves howling. But the wolves are only keeping in touch with each other or telling other packs they are there.

Town and country

The cunning red fox has learned to change its habits to suit its surroundings. Now it is as happy living in towns as in the countryside.

High jumps
Foxes can catch small animals by springing into the air and pouncing on them. The fox pins its victim to the ground with its front paws

Taking out the trash
Garbage cans are good places for the streetwise fox to find a meal. But it should learn to clean up after it eats!

Safe at home
When cubs are due, the vixen, or mother fox, looks for a hole underground to give birth. The fox's home is called an earth, and the cubs can stay safe inside.

Lofty perch
The red fox is not an expert climber, but it climbs well enough to find a safe place to sleep after a night out hunting.

Fox about town
More and more foxes are seen in towns. They live in large gardens and parks or near railway lines, and make their earths in sheds, cellars, and drainpipes.

A useful brush
A fox's tail is called a brush, but it is not used for sweeping the floor. The mother fox flicks her tail to warn her cubs of danger, and a tail makes a cozy blanket in chilly weather.

Autumn feast

Foxes are happy to eat fruit when meat is in short supply. Juicy berries are hard to resist – and much easier to catch than run-away mice.

This red fox is about 3½ feet long from the tip of its nose to the tip of its tail

Lone ranger

A red fox hunts on its own. But related female red foxes may help each other to look after cubs.

Life on ice

Temperatures in the Arctic can fall so low that humans would quickly freeze. But animals such as the Arctic fox are specially designed to survive the severe cold.

Deep freeze
Arctic foxes like to keep a store of food buried for times when prey is scarce. One fox was found with forty birds and over thirty eggs in the "freezer."

Snow-white fox
Arctic foxes have thick, soft fur to keep them warm. In winter their gray coats usually change to white. They are then perfectly hidden in the snowy landscape.

Table scraps
As well as hunting for themselves, Arctic foxes often tag along behind polar bears and pick up some of the bears' leftovers.

Summer clothes
This Arctic fox is wearing its smoky gray summer suit. When the snow melts in the spring, the fox does not need to be white anymore.

Short, rounded ears lose less heat than long ears

This Arctic fox is about 1 foot tall

Alarm call

A lemming hibernating under the snow may get a nasty shock if a hungry Arctic fox sniffs it out. The fox reaches the lemming by jumping up and down to break the ice.

Winter diet

The Arctic wolf is a type of gray wolf with rounded ears and, usually, a white coat. Most of the time it hunts moose and caribou, but in winter, when food is scarce, it sometimes has to settle for smaller prey, like this Arctic hare.

Feet are lined with fur to save heat

New arrivals

As spring arrives, many animals settle in one place to raise a family.

Hot dogs

Y ou may think that dogs could not possibly live in hot or dry places like tropical forests or deserts, but they do. Some are hardly ever seen.

Trapped in fur

A fox cannot take off its coat when it is too hot. So the kit fox, like many other animals that live in hot places, has big ears which let body heat escape.

This Ruppell's fox is about 18 inches long with a 12-inch tail

Secret hunter

Few people have seen the small-eared zorro. It lives only in the Amazon rain forest of South America. It hunts for food on its own – and only at night.

Out of the sun

The fennec fox is the smallest fox in the world. It lives in the Sahara Desert, where it rests under rocks to hide from the heat of the day. In the cooler evenings, the fox comes out to hunt for insects.

Foot pads

Foxes that live in deserts have fur-lined feet, so they can walk across the hot sand or rock without burning their toes.

Hot snacks

The Australian outback can be very hot and dry. It may look lifeless, but dingoes can usually find something to eat. This one has found a monitor lizard in one of the water holes.

Large ears for hearing and keeping cool

Well-hidden

The brownish-gray coat of Blanford's fox helps it hide among the rocks where it lives. Blanford's fox is one of four kinds of desert foxes. The others are the pale, Ruppell's, and the fennec.

Furry fox

Ruppell's fox lives in stony or sandy deserts. Its sand-colored coat looks soft and thick – and it is!

Howls and growls

Woofs and barks don't mean much to us, but dogs understand them. Each kind of dog has its own language, which varies from pack to pack.

Monkeying around

When African wild dogs are playing, they often whimper or chatter. They can sound very un-doglike and much more like monkeys.

Baby talk

A wolf is never too young to howl! Gray wolf pups call to their friends too.

A far cry

A pack of howling wolves can be heard by humans as far as 10 miles away. All the members of the pack join in. Other packs in the area (almost 200 square miles) will get the message to stay away.

Howdy, coyote

A howling coyote stars in many westerns. Its call is a series of yelps and a long wail. It's not trying to scare cowboys. It's only claiming its territory.

Dog with no bark

Dingoes may look like ordinary dogs, but unlike them, dingoes hardly ever bark! They howl and yelp and make all sorts of other noises instead.

Whistle stop

You may have heard of a dog whistle, but have you heard of a whistling dog? Dholes often whistle to the rest of the pack when they want to regroup after a failed hunt.

Telling the neighbors

The gray fox often climbs trees – an unusual habit for a fox – and is also called the tree fox. It's no secret when a gray fox is ready to mate. Its piercing screams reach every fox in its territory.

This handsome gray fox is about 15 inches tall at the shoulder

When climbing, the front paws grip, the back paws push

The pack goes hunting

Most wolves and wild dogs live in packs. They travel, rest, and hunt together. The pack is led by the strongest and bravest individuals – and they may have to prove it.

Stalking

Once African wild dogs are within 160 feet of their prey, they begin to stalk, ears back and head lowered. When the chase begins, the dogs can keep running for 2 or 3 miles at about 30 mph.

Hanging on

With a powerful leap, the lead dog jumps at the nose or throat of the fleeing animal. The dog will hang on, no matter what, until the other dogs come to help it.

Home on the range

Each pack of wolves or wild dogs claims its own territory to hunt in. The dogs spray a scent so every dog knows its own and other packs' territories. A territory can be up to 580 square miles – nearly twice the size of New York City.

Baby food

After a kill, adults bring food back for the pups. This may be a piece of skin or a bone, or the dogs may regurgitate (bring up) meat they've already chewed, which is easier for young pups to eat.

Nose to tail

When hunting in freezing snow, wolves walk in single file. They take turns in the lead and make tracks for the others to walk in.

Eating alone

Jackals may hunt in family groups for large animals. But sometimes they make it clear they would rather be alone at mealtime!

A family affair

A pack of African wild dogs can total more than 60 animals, but the average number is 10. All the males, and usually all the females, are related.

This African wild dog is about 2 feet tall

Amazing senses

Dogs survive by using their senses, especially sight, hearing, and smell. With their senses they can tell friend from foe, find food, and leave and pick up messages.

Scratch and sniff

Wolves mark trees on their trails with urine, just as pet dogs do. A male wolf will often scrape a mark on the ground too, so that other wolves will see that it's his trail even if they don't smell it.

Ears to the ground

Dogs have much better hearing than humans. If you were a fox or a wolf, you would be able to hear a watch ticking 30 feet away. This bat-eared fox can hear insects moving.

Past master

A dog does not have photographs to give it a picture of the past. It uses its strong sense of smell to find out who has been there before it.

Touching scene

Mouths and teeth are fierce tools for catching food, but they are also used gently for carrying pups or for grooming. This jackal family shows affection by grooming each other.

This raccoon dog is about 8 inches high – a bit taller than a pencil

What big ears you have!

In the fairy tale of Little Red Riding Hood, the big bad wolf pretends to be the little girl's grandmother. But he finds it hard to disguise his large ears and eyes.

This raccoon dog looks as if it has a black mask on its face – just like a raccoon

Sensible dog

The raccoon dog obviously feels the cold. It is the only dog that sleeps through much of the winter. This is called hibernating.

Wide-eyed

The fennec fox has large eyes and it can see in the dark. This is useful to the fox when it's out at night, hunting for insects and other small animals for its dinner.

Dogs in danger

Living in the wild is not always easy. For some dogs it has become a struggle to survive. Some catch diseases, some have their homes destroyed by people, and many are hunted for their fur.

Stop, thief!
Simien jackals of Ethiopia (Africa) are nearly extinct, as farmers take over the land where the jackals live and hunt for food.

Driven out
People have taken over much of the grassland home of the African wild dog, leaving swamps and deserts for it to hunt in. With too little food, many wild dogs have died.

Wolf watch
The red wolf is almost extinct. People are trying to help red wolves increase their numbers by breeding them in zoos. When the puppies can look after themselves they are placed in the wild.

Tree den
The short-legged bush dog is very rare. It lives in groups of up to ten and makes its den in burrows or hollow trees.

Forest dogs
Asian red dholes live in rain forests. But these forests are being cut down to make farmland, leaving fewer places where the dholes can live.

Whose coat is it?
Many foxes, wolves, jackals, and other dogs are dying out because they are hunted by people. Some are killed by farmers who think they are a nuisance, and many are killed to make fur coats.

Oil or nothing

San Joaquin kit foxes live among the oil fields of California and are surrounded by cotton farms. There are only about 7,000 of these kit foxes left.

In name only

The rare maned wolf of central South America is not a wolf. It was given the name because of its large size, and it is often described as a fox on stilts! If it is scared by an enemy, it raises its long mane to make itself look bigger.

This maned wolf is about 30 inches high at the shoulder

25

New arrivals

Young wolves, dogs, and foxes may not have to go to school, but they still have a lot of learning and growing to do before they can look after themselves.

Born blind
Puppies are born blind. A newborn red fox is about the size of a mole. It has short fluffy fur and cuddles up to its mother to keep warm.

Too young
This gray wolf cub is about eight weeks old. He will not join the rest of the pack on a hunting trip until he is six months old.

This young wolf cub is about 14 inches tall

Wolf protector

In legend, Romulus and Remus were twin brothers brought up by a wolf. She must have taught them well – Romulus founded the city of Rome, Italy, in 753 B.C.

Mother's milk

At first, puppies drink only their mother's milk, just as human babies do. Mother's milk is good for the pups and builds their strength.

Meat eaters

When they are only a few weeks old, African wild dogs get a taste for meat. They love to eat pieces regurgitated by their parents.

Rough and tumble

Rolling and tumbling together is good fun – and good practice for life as an adult. If there aren't any brothers or sisters to play with, Mom will usually do!

A long way to go

Puppies have smaller ears, shorter noses, and shorter legs than adults. The legs of a maned wolf pup have to grow a lot before the pup looks like its parents!

A helping paw

Young jackals often stay to help look after newborn brothers and sisters before leaving home. More puppies survive if the mother has help, and the helper can learn things that might be useful when it raises its own family.

Best friends

Pet dogs are descended from wolves. Humans and wolves became hunting companions as long ago as the Stone Age. Dogs have been helping humans hunt and herd for thousands of years.

Sheep leaper
The kelpie from Australia is partly descended from the wild dingo. It has an unusual way of moving among the sheep. It leaps on the sheeps' backs and runs around on top of their fleece!

Smelly job
The German shepherd has been bred to look like its wolf ancestors. It has a good sense of smell and is often used by the police to sniff out explosives and drugs.

Call of the wild
Some dogs have returned to living in the wild. Pariah dogs of Asia usually scavenge around villages, but they are not owned by anyone and they live and breed like wild animals.

Dog power
The husky is a wolflike dog with a thick woolly coat. It pulls sleds across the snow and helps with hunting and herding. In North America it also pulls sleds in races. This husky is about 2 feet tall.

Dog god

The ancient Egyptians used dogs for hunting. They also had a god called Anubis who they believed was half dog and half jackal.

Born for battle

Many breeds of dog developed in ancient times. For example, the mastiff was bred from fierce dogs as a guard dog, and the greyhound was bred from fast dogs for hunting.

Out hunting

A bull terrier may not look like a wolf but it has a hunting instinct like a wolf's, handed down to it from its wild ancestors. It would probably love to join some friends on a hunting trip – if it was allowed to!

29

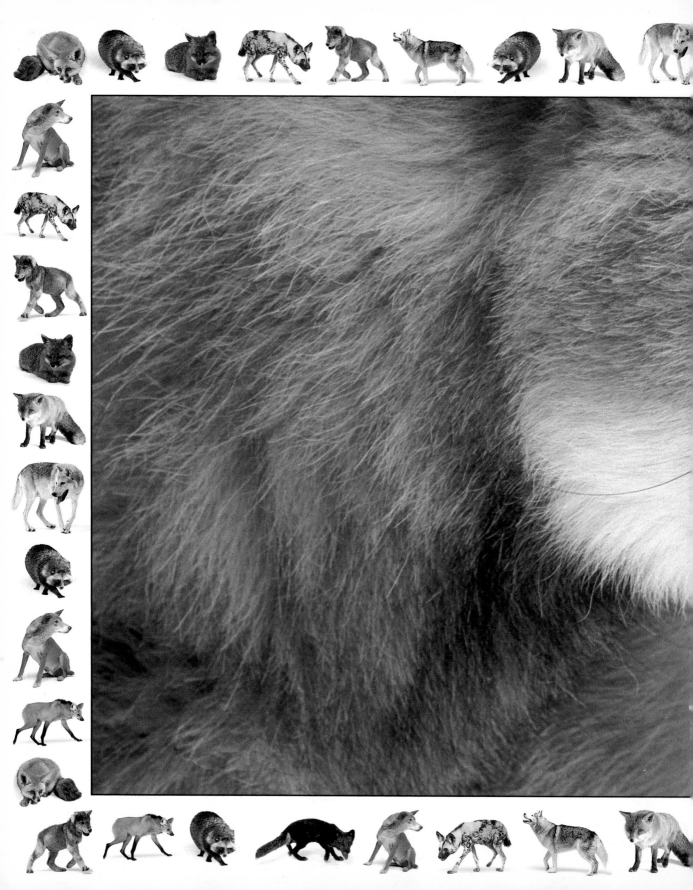